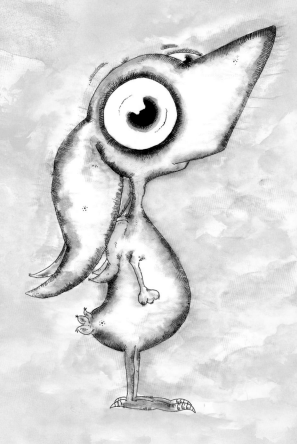

Wince, The Monster of Worry

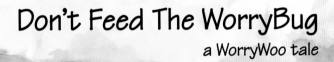

Don't Feed The WorryBug
a WorryWoo tale

by Andi Green

Printed with Soy Ink
ISBN 978-0-9792860-4-9

To see all The WorryWoo Monsters™
go to www.WorryWoos.com

Printed in China

This book is dedicated to
Jeff and Penny.
Thank you for finding me.

On a bench in a park on a bright sunny day,
Wince, The Monster of Worry, let time slip away.

He looked at the clock—it was a

quarter past two—

Time Flies Watch Repair

when Wince started to think about **all** he must do.

He had homework

and laundry,

he needed clean pants,

he must bake some cookies for the WorryWoo dance!

Then Wince started to wonder—
Did he leave the light on?
Was his backside too poofy?

Where had **all** his friends gone?

And his worries kept

growing

'til he heard a soft *buzz*

that made goose bumps appear...

for he knew what **it** was.

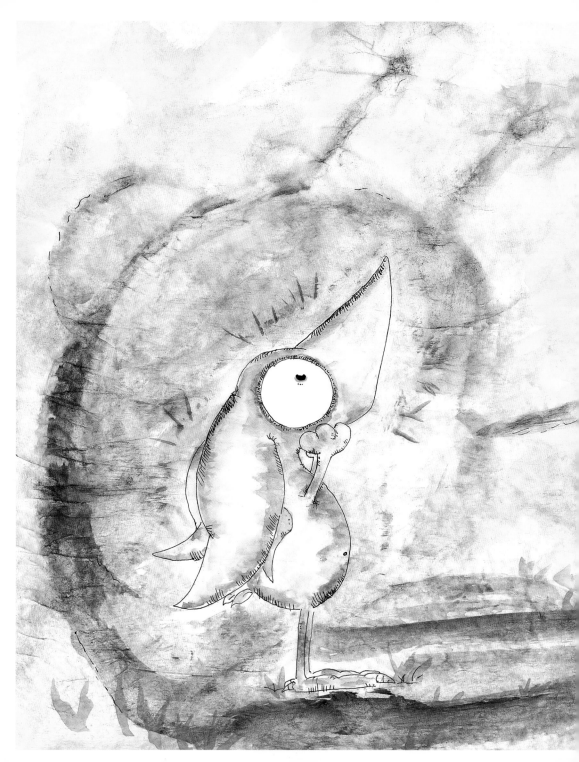

There was only **one** creature
that made such a sound,
around monsters that worry
it could often be found.

Some call it
the WorryBug
and this is for sure—

if you feed it a worry,
it will always want **more.**

Buzz Buzz

Wince heard as its noisy wings flapped.

It flew up and down as he shooed and he clapped.

It flittered and fluttered around Wince's ear.

In the **blink** of an eye...

more worries appeared!

Did he feed his fish, Ted?

Did his dog get a bone?

Did he send all his WooMail?

Did he bring his bike home?

And with every new worry that came Wince's way, the WorryBug shouted, "HIP, HIP HOORAY!"

For the more that Wince worried,

the more the bug **grew**;

it nibbled and **munched** on

his worry-filled stew.

Wince said to the WorryBug:

"Perhaps you should leave?"

He asked quite politely... and even used PLEASE.

Yet the WorryBug stayed, for the two of them knew
that Wince would still worry, that's what he would do.

As day turned to night, Wince got ready for bed.

The WorryBug YAWNED and laid next to his head.

But its buzzing kept Wince from going to sleep,

so he tossed and he turned

and he tried to count sheep.

While thoughts of What if,
Could be, Maybe and Might

made Wince
worry more...
he was worried all night!

When morning arrived, Wince looked up and

GASPED!

The WorryBug had grown...

it had happened so fast.

It used to be tiny,
an annoyance quite small.

Now it covered his kitchen,
the ceiling and wall.

The bug's belly **gurgled**—full of worries it was.

No longer could Wince sweep it under the rug.

Its buzzing went on and Wince started to fret

about all of the things that hadn't happened just yet.

No cookies were baked,
the laundry had piled;
Wince hadn't done homework
in such a long while!

"Enough!"

Wince exclaimed.
"There must be a way
to get rid of a WorryBug.
It can no longer stay."

about catapults, cranes,
wagons and goats.

He plotted and mapped out
a WorryBug graph,

then called in the EXPERTS
...The WorryBug Staff!

Together they studied this big, growing beast
and built a bug net out of Wince's bed sheets.

They were having such fun, Wince was worried no more,

and soon he was baking and doing his chores.

But just when Wince thought
his work was complete,
the WorryBug buzzed,

"I need something to eat!"

Wince looked at the bug—it was once again small—
for while Wince had been busy,
he hadn't worried at all.

"You've ignored me all day," the tiny bug said,
"and you haven't been worried, so I haven't been fed!"

Then the bug stomped its feet and buzzed all the more...

Wince took a **firm** stand
and showed it the door.

"I've got things to do—I must work, I must play!

I'M NOT GOING TO WORRY,

so go on your way!"

Buzz Buzz

Wince heard as the bug flew about,
still trying to make one last worry come out.

It flittered and fluttered around Wince's ear,
yet Wince wouldn't give in and it soon
disappeared.

Wince knew very well that this wasn't the end.
The bug **might** be back if he worried again.

But Wince would be ready, should he hear that *BUZZ BUZZ,*

to say "NO" to the WorryBug simply because...

Wince had learned that

his worries got **bigger** each day,

when he allowed the WorryBug to nibble away.

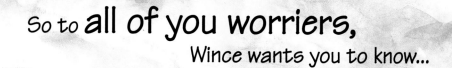

So to **all of you worriers,**
Wince wants you to know...

Don't feed the WorryBug,

or your worries will grow!

the end

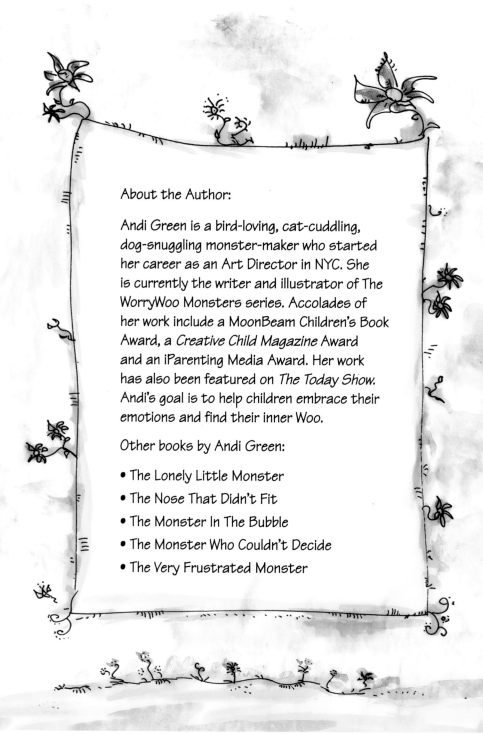

About the Author:

Andi Green is a bird-loving, cat-cuddling, dog-snuggling monster-maker who started her career as an Art Director in NYC. She is currently the writer and illustrator of The WorryWoo Monsters series. Accolades of her work include a MoonBeam Children's Book Award, a *Creative Child Magazine* Award and an iParenting Media Award. Her work has also been featured on *The Today Show*. Andi's goal is to help children embrace their emotions and find their inner Woo.

Other books by Andi Green:

- The Lonely Little Monster
- The Nose That Didn't Fit
- The Monster In The Bubble
- The Monster Who Couldn't Decide
- The Very Frustrated Monster